The Little Old Toymaker

and

Other Stories

by
ENID BLYTON

Illustrated by
Peter Wilks

AWARD PUBLICATIONS LIMITED

For further information on Enid Blyton please contact
www.blyton.com

ISBN 0-86163-930-8

First published 1998
3rd impression 2000

Published by Award Publications Limited,
27 Longford Street, London NW1 3DZ

Printed in Singapore

CONTENTS

The Little Old Toymaker

There was once a little old man who lived with his wife in a tiny cottage. He was called Stubby the toymaker, and he could make the loveliest toys. He liked making tiny toys the best – small chairs and tables for doll's-houses, little beds for tiny dolls to sleep in, and things like that. He was very clever at mending broken dolls too. Whenever a doll's face was broken, or an arm or leg, it was brought to Stubby and he mended it lovingly.

Then came a sad time for the old toymaker. Nobody seemed to want his toys any more. All the children had unbreakable dolls which never needed mending. People said his shop was old-fashioned, and they went to the big new stores in the nearest town. Stubby went on making his little chairs and tables, but nobody bought them.

"Stubby, dear, I don't know what we shall do," said his little old wife. "We have no money now, you know. You have not sold anything for two weeks. I cannot buy flour to make bread if I have no money."

"Dear me, wife, this will never do!" said Stubby, taking off his big round glasses and polishing them furiously. He always did that when he wanted to think hard, and right now he was thinking very hard indeed.

"Have you thought of an idea, Stubby?" asked his wife at last. Stubby nodded.

"Yes," he said. "But it isn't a very good one. You know, wife, our shop window is very old and the glass is not good. Perhaps people cannot see my nice little toys very well through it. Suppose we set out some little chairs and tables and beds on the broad top of the old wall outside. Then everyone would see them!"

"That is a very good idea," said his

wife. "I am quite sure that if people saw them, they would buy them. You really do make them so beautifully, Stubby dear."

So out went the old toymaker and placed six little red chairs and a table to match on the top of the low stone wall outside. Then he put two small beds there as well, and his wife arranged the tiny sheets, blankets and pillows on each. They did look so sweet! The sun shone down on them and old Stubby felt quite certain that anyone passing by would come in and buy them at once!

But nobody did. Nobody even seemed to notice the tiny furniture. It was most disappointing.

"I'll go and fetch them in after we've had supper," said Stubby. So the two sat down and had a poor supper of one cooked turnip out of the garden and a crust of stale bread. It was nearly dark when they had finished. Stubby got up and went out into the little garden to fetch in his dolls' furniture.

He walked to the wall and looked down at it in the twilight. To his great astonishment there was no furniture there! It had gone! He felt all along the wall in dismay, and then hurried back to his wife.

"Wife, wife!" he called. "All my chairs and the table and beds are gone!"

"Has someone stolen them?" said his wife, almost in tears. "Oh, what a shameful thing to steal from a poor old couple like ourselves!"

"Never mind," said Stubby. "It shows someone noticed them, anyhow. I'll put some more out tomorrow and I'll keep my eye on them!"

So the next day he put out a set of green chairs and a table to match, and one tiny bed. He sat at his window and watched to see that no one took them. But nobody seemed to notice them at all.

And then a strange thing happened. Stubby could hardly believe his eyes! He saw the chairs and table and bed walking off by themselves! Yes, really – they just slid down the wall and made off out of the gate!

Stubby ran after them. "Hi! Hi!" he called. "What do you think you're doing?"

He made a grab at a chair – and to his enormous surprise, he got hold of a little wriggling figure that he couldn't see!

"Let me go, let me go!" screamed the little creature he couldn't see.

"Show yourself then," commanded Stubby, shaking with excitement. At once the little struggling creature showed himself and became visible. It was a very small pixie!

"Bless us all!" said Stubby, his eyes nearly dropping out with amazement. "It's the very first time I've ever seen a fairy! Pray what are you doing, stealing my chairs?"

"Oh, are they yours?" said the pixie, in surprise. "Hi, brothers. Stop carrying off this furniture. It belongs to someone!"

At once all the chairs and tables were set down, and many small pixies became visible before Stubby's astonished eyes.

"We are really very sorry," said the first pixie. "You see, we found the chairs, tables, and beds on the wall there, and we

didn't know they belonged to anyone at all. We thought they were very beautiful, so we took them into the woods to show the Queen."

"Dear, dear me!" said Stubby, flattered and pleased. "Did you really think they were beautiful? And what did the Queen think?"

"Oh, she liked them so much she said she would like ever so many more," said the pixies. "She has a new country house, you know, and she has been looking everywhere for furniture nice enough for it."

"Well!" said Stubby, most excited, "this is really lovely. You might tell the Queen that I have a great deal more furniture if she would like to see it. I didn't put out my best pieces in case it rained."

"Oh, of course we'll tell her," said the pixies. "Goodbye for the present, old man. Take your chairs, and table, and bed – we'll go and tell the Queen all you have said."

Off they went, and Stubby took his toy furniture into the cottage with him and told his surprised wife all that had happened.

That night there came a knocking at his door – and when Stubby opened it, who do you suppose was there? Yes! – the Queen, all dressed in shining moonlight with a silver star in her hair! She sat on the table and asked Stubby to show her all the furniture he had.

With shaking hands the old man set it out, and the Queen exclaimed in delight. "Oh, what beautiful things you make!" she cried. "Just the right size for the little folk too. I suppose, old man, you are too busy to make things for us? The humans must be so pleased with your work that you will have no time for fairy folk."

Then Stubby told the Queen how hard he found it to sell anything, and his wife told her how little they had in the larder.

"We would be so glad if you could buy some of our goods," she said.

"I can do better than that!" cried the beautiful Queen in delight. "Stubby, come and live in Fairyland, will you? Please do! You can make all the furniture for my new country house. And there are no end of little jobs that your clever fingers could do really beautifully. I believe you could even patch up the wings of pixies when they get torn!"

"Oh yes, I could!" said Stubby, his eyes shining brightly behind his big spectacles. "I'll come whenever you wish, Your Majesty!"

So Stubby and his wife left their little cottage one fine morning and went to Fairyland. There the Queen gave them a little white house on a hill, with two pixies for servants. Stubby makes beautiful furniture all day long, and he often patches up the torn wings of the pixies.

And once a month he dresses himself up very grandly indeed, and so does his wife. For then the Queen herself comes to tea, and each time there is a new little chair for her to sit in. She is so pleased.

The Three Lovely Presents

Father was going away for a whole week and the three children were sad. They hated it when their father went away.

"Mummy will miss you," said Janet.

"So will we," said Dan.

"We'll love to see you back on Saturday," said Rosy, and they all gave their father a hug.

"I shall bring back three lovely presents for your garden!" he said.

"What will you bring?" asked Dan.

"I shall bring a new wheelbarrow, a fine digging-spade and a green watering-can!" said Father.

"Good!" said Dan, who longed for a spade to dig up his garden.

"Lovely!" said Janet, who had always wanted a wheelbarrow.

"Oooh!" said Rosy, who simply loved watering her flowers. They were all good gardeners and had little gardens of their own.

"Goodbye," said Father. "Be good, and help Mummy all you can!" Then he jumped into his car, started it, and off he went down the road.

Mother was going to be very busy while Father was away. She was going to do some spring-cleaning!

"You can really help me a lot," she said to the children. "And Daddy will be so pleased to see everything shining and bright when he gets home."

But, dear me, when Mother found something she wanted Dan to do, he sulked and wouldn't do it! It was when Mother found that she had come to the end of her soap powder, and she asked Dan to run down to the shops and get her some more.

"I'm busy reading," sulked Dan. "You always ask me to do errands while I'm reading, Mummy."

"Will you go for me, Janet?" said Mother, looking rather sad.

But Janet was busy too. She was washing her dolls' dresses. "Can't I go when I've finished this?" she said.

Rosy was busy tidying the toy-cupboard. She looked up. "Mummy, I'll go!" she said. "It won't take me a minute." And it didn't. She popped on her coat, ran down the road, and was back in minutes with the soap powder. Her mother was very pleased.

The next day Mother wanted some daffodils picked out of the garden and put into a vase for the table, because Aunt Ellen was coming to tea and she

wanted her table to look nice.

"Janet dear, run and pick some daffies for me!" she said.

"Oh bother!" said Janet.

"Well, perhaps Dan will go," said Mother.

But Dan was far too busy. Rosy jumped up and said never mind, she would go. So down the garden she went and picked a large bunch of daffodils. She arranged them beautifully in a vase and put them on the table. As she did so she trod on Janet's toe, quite by accident.

"Oh, you clumsy girl!" cried Janet. "Look where you're going! I shan't lend you my new wheelbarrow if you're not careful!"

"Sorry," said Rosy. "You shouldn't stick your feet out so far."

That night everybody forgot to put Sandy the dog into his kennel, and Mother suddenly remembered just as it was the children's bedtime.

"Oh dear!" she said. "We've forgotten Sandy! Who will take the torch and put him into his kennel for me?"

Dan said nothing; he didn't like the dark. Janet thought it was raining and she didn't want to go out. So Rosy thought she had better find the torch and take Sandy, or else her mother would have to do it.

"You're very selfish," she said to Dan

as she went to find the torch. "You just don't do anything."

"If you talk to me like that, you shan't use my new spade when Daddy brings it," said Dan sharply.

"I don't care," said Rosy. "I shall have my new watering-can!" She found the torch and ran out in the dark with Sandy. It wasn't raining, and there was a lovely moon, so she didn't need the torch after all. Sandy went into his kennel and curled up on his blanket.

The next day Pussy was very naughty. She jumped up on the table when nobody was in the room, and began to drink the milk out of the jug there. When Janet came into the room Pussy was frightened and jumped down. But her claws caught in the tablecloth and down it came, and all the tea-things with it. The milk spilled all over the floor, and the jam-pot broke. Oh, what a mess of plates and milk and jam!

"Mummy! Mummy!" shouted Janet. "Pussy has knocked over all the tea-things!"

"Oh, Janet!" cried her mother. "What a nuisance! Do clear up the mess, like a good girl, because I'm in the middle of putting up new curtains in your room, and I just want to finish them."

Janet looked at the mess and sulked. Why should she have to clear up what Pussy had spilt? She was just going out to play, and it would take a long time to clear everything. Then she saw Dan coming in, and she called to him.

"Dan! Look what Pussy's done! I'm just going out, and Mummy wants all this cleared up. Will you do it?" And before Dan could say yes or no, the naughty little girl had run out to play next door. Dan stared at the mess and frowned.

"I'm jolly well not going to clear this up," he thought. "Why should I? Mummy will easily clear it up when she comes down."

So Dan slipped out too, and went to play with George, who had a new railway set, over the road.

Soon Rosy came in – and when she

saw the dreadful mess all over the dining-room, she did get a shock.

"Oh dear!" she said. "I suppose Pussy has done this! I'd better clear up the things in case Mummy comes down and gets upset."

So Rosy picked up all the tea-things,

wiped up the spilt milk and the jam, and tried to mend the jam-pot with glue. Then she washed up all the dirty things, and cleared everything away neatly.

Mother didn't come downstairs until all the children were back again, and were sitting at the table doing their homework. She was so pleased when she saw the upset tea-things cleared away.

"Thank you, Janet," she said gratefully. "It was good of you to clear up the mess of spilt milk and jam and put everything away."

Janet went red. "I didn't clear it up," she said, surprised. "I told Dan to. I was just going out."

Then it was Dan's turn to go red. For Mother turned to him and said, "Thank you, Dan, dear. That was very kind of you."

"I didn't do it," said Dan, but he wished he had.

"I did it, Mummy," said Rosy, looking up from her spelling. "It didn't take me a minute."

"You're a real help to me, Rosy," said her mother, and she kissed her. Janet and Dan were still red. They wished that she had kissed them too.

Well, the next excitement was Father coming home again! The three children were all at the window watching for the car, and at last it drew up at the gate. Janet gave a shriek of delight.

"Look at the parcels in the back! I can see my wheelbarrow with its one wheel sticking out. And it's got a rubber tyre on!"

"And I can see the handle of my spade!" shouted Dan, running to the door.

"And I can see the spout of my watering-can!" cried Rosy; and out they all ran to welcome their father. He came in with all the presents and his suitcase. He hugged everybody and asked Mother how she was.

"Splendid," said Mother. "And all the

spring-cleaning is done. So I have had a very good week."

"And have the children helped you?" asked Father.

Mother looked rather solemn. "Well," she said, "I've had a lot of things done for me. I ran out of soap powder and somebody ran down to the shops and fetched it for me."

"Good," said Father. "Who was that?"

"Rosy!" said Mother, and Father gave her a hug.

"Then I wanted some daffies picked and put into a vase when Aunt Ellen came to tea," said Mother, "and somebody did them most beautifully for me, without a single grumble."

"Fine!" said Father, looking at Dan and Janet and wondering which of them it was. "Who was that?"

"Rosy!" said Mother, and Rosy got another hug. Then Mother went on: "And one night we forgot all about putting Sandy into his kennel, so somebody got the torch and went out to put him in for me."

"Splendid!" said Father. "I wonder who that was?"

"Rosy!" said Mother, and Rosy got a kiss. "And another time Pussy jumped on the table and upset all the things on to the floor," said Mother. "Somebody cleared them all up without being asked – though the somebody who was asked didn't do it!"

"And who was the somebody who did it without being asked?" said Father. "Was it Rosy again?"

"It was," said Mother, and Rosy got such a hug that she lost her breath. "Rosy has been the greatest help to me, but I'm afraid the others haven't really tried. Isn't it a pity?"

"A great pity," said Father, undoing the three lovely presents he had bought. "I'm afraid Rosy must have all the garden things! Rosy, here is the spade, and the wheelbarrow and the watering-can, with my love and best thanks for being good to Mummy for me while I was away."

Janet and Dan burst into tears. "But,

Daddy, you promised you would bring us those!" wept Janet.

"Yes, I promised to bring the presents," said Daddy, "but I didn't say who was going to have them! And as you have done nothing to deserve them, Rosy must have them all!"

So Rosy did; but you know she really is a most unselfish little girl, for she lets Dan use the lovely big spade, and she lets Janet have the wheelbarrow whenever she asks for it. Don't you think that's nice of her?

The Cross
Little Tadpole

Once upon a time a big mass of jelly lay on the top of a pond. In it were tiny black specks, like little black commas.

The sun shone down and warmed the jelly. A fish tried to nibble a bit, but it was too slippery. A big black beetle tried a little too, but he didn't like it. The rain came and pattered down on the jelly.

Every day the tiny black specks grew bigger. They were eggs. Soon it would be time for them to hatch and swim about in the pond as tadpoles.

The day came when the black eggs had become wriggling tadpoles and then the jelly began to disappear. It was no longer needed. It had saved the eggs from being eaten, because it was too slippery for any creature to gobble up for its dinner. It had helped to hold the eggs up to the sunshine too. But now it was of no more use.

The little black wrigglers swam to a waterweed and held on to it. They were very tiny. When they were hungry they nibbled the weed. It tasted nice to them.

They grew bigger each day in the pond, and soon the other creatures began to know them. "There go two tadpoles!" said the stickleback, with all his spines standing up along his back.

"Funny creatures, aren't they?" said the big black beetle. "All head and tail – nothing much else to them!"

"Hundreds of them!" said the water-snail. "The whole pond is full of them."

"I like them for my dinner," said the

dragonfly grub. "Look – I hide down here in the mud, and when I see a nice fat tadpole swimming by, out I pounce and catch one in my jaws."

A good many of the tadpoles were eaten by enemies because they were not clever enough or fast enough to escape. Those that were left grew big and raced about the pond, wriggling their long tails swiftly.

One little tadpole had some narrow escapes. One of the black beetles nearly caught him – in fact, a tiny piece was bitten off his tail. Another time he

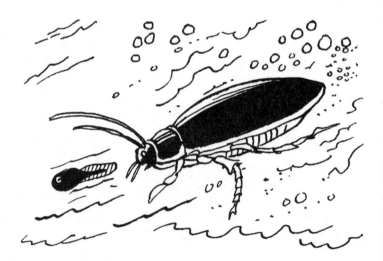

scraped himself badly on the spines of the stickleback. And twice the dragonfly grub darted at him and almost caught him. Each time the little tadpole was very cross.

"Leave me alone! What harm am I doing to you? I don't want to be your dinner!"

The pond had other things in it besides the fish, the grubs, and the beetles. It had some frogs, and the little tadpole was always in a temper about these.

"Those big fat frogs are so rude and bad-mannered," he said to the other tadpoles. "How I hate them with their gaping mouths and great big eyes!"

The frogs didn't like the cross little tadpole because he called rude names after them. Sometimes they chased him, swimming fast with their strong hind legs.

"If we catch you, we shall spank you hard!" they croaked. The tadpole swam behind a stone and called back to them, "Old croakers! Old greedy-mouths! Old stick-out eyes!"

The frogs tried to overturn the stone and get at the rude tadpole. But he burrowed down in the mud, and came up far behind them.

"Old croakers !" he cried. "Here I am – peep-bo! Old croakers!"

The frogs lay in wait for the rude tadpole. He never knew when a fat green frog would jump into the water from the bank, almost on top of him. He never knew when one would scramble out of the mud just below him.

"I'm tired of these frogs," he told the other tadpoles. "I wish somebody would eat them. I wish those ducks would come back and gobble them up!"

The tadpole had never forgotten one day when some wild ducks had flown down to the pond, and had frightened all the frogs and other creatures very much indeed.

The ducks had caught and eaten three frogs, and at least twenty tadpoles. It had been a dreadful day. None of the tadpoles ever forgot it.

"You shouldn't wish for those ducks to come back!" said the stickleback. "You might be eaten yourself!"

"I'm getting too big to be eaten," said the cross tadpole. "Stickleback, what else eats frogs?"

"The grass snake eats frogs," said the

pretty little stickleback. "I once saw him come sliding down into the water. He swam beautifully. He ate four frogs when he came."

"I've a good mind to go and tell him to come to this pond and eat some more frogs," said the tadpole. "He might be glad to know there was a good meal here for him."

"Well, he is lying in the sun on the bank of the pond over there," said the stickleback. "Go and tell him now! But, tadpole – listen to me – I don't think I have ever met anyone quite so silly as you in all my life!"

"Pooh!" said the tadpole rudely, and swam off towards the bank on which the long grass snake was lying, curled up in a heap.

The tadpole poked his black head out of the water and called to the snake, "Hi, grass snake! Can you hear me?"

The snake woke up in surprise. He looked at the tadpole. "What do you want?" he said.

"I've come to tell you that there are a

this warm pond. Most of those horrid frogs have gone now, so life is very pleasant."

"There's your friend the grass snake," said the stickleback, poking his head up suddenly. "Why don't you go and tell him to come and gobble up all the frogs in this pond, as you said you would?"

The tadpole was just about to leap off his bit of wood when he caught sight of himself in the water. The pond was calm that day, like a mirror, and the tadpole could see himself well.

He stared down at himself in horror and amazement – for he did not see a tadpole, but a small frog!

"I've turned into a frog!" he croaked. "I have, I have! And all the other tadpoles are little frogs too! Why didn't I notice that before?"

"Tadpoles always turn into frogs. I could have told you that before, but you never would listen to anyone," said the stickleback. "Well – are you going to find the grass snake and tell him to come and eat you and all your friends too? You said you would tell him where the frogs were in this pond."

But the tiny frog did not go to tell the snake anything. He felt quite certain that he would be eaten at once. He jumped into the pond with a splash and swam as fast as he could to the other side of the water.

Wasn't he a silly fellow? He is five years old now, and quite grown up – but you have only to say "Snake" to him to send him leaping away in fright!

Bottom of the Class!

Somebody always has to be at the bottom of every class. "But," said Miss Brown, "it needn't always be the same person, Bobby!"

You see, Bobby was always at the bottom. He was very sorry about it, but he couldn't help it. He had been ill for two years of his school life, and that meant that he was far behind everyone else.

He wasn't very good at craftwork, either, because he was left-handed, and that seemed to make him awkward with the tools that the class used to make things.

He was bad at games because he wasn't strong and couldn't run fast. His mother was often very sorry for the little boy, because he never once grumbled or complained, and yet she knew he must be unhappy about it.

But there was one thing that Bobby was very, very fond of, and that was gardening. He might not be able to run fast, but you should see him weeding! And the flowers didn't mind whether he was left-handed or right-handed, because he always knew when to water them, when to weed, and when to tie them up so that the wind couldn't blow them down.

"You know, Paul," his mother said to his father, "Bobby isn't much good at anything except gardening. So we must help him all we can with that. When people aren't much good at anything, and can't help it, it's very important to find something they like and can do really well. And gardening is what Bobby likes best of all."

So his parents gave Bobby a very big piece of the garden. They bought him a spade and fork, a watering-can, trowels, dibbers, twine for tying, and

a fine wheelbarrow. He was delighted.

"Oh, thank you!" he said. "Now I'll really be able to grow marvellous flowers. And, Mummy, do you know what I shall do? I shall grow enough flowers for you to have them all over the house, and enough to take to Miss Brown twice a week to keep our classroom beautiful. Then she'll know that even if I'm at the bottom of the class and stay there, I can at least do something!"

He kept his word. He worked hard in his garden each day. He dug, he weeded, he sowed, he watered. He thinned out his seedlings, he hunted for slugs, he tied up his tall plants so that the wind should not break them.

And all the term his mother had her house full of flowers from Bobby's garden, and, really, you should have seen Bobby's classroom! There were roses on Miss Brown's desk, lupins on the window-sill, pinks on the bookcase smelling as sweet as sugar. Miss Brown said they never had so many lovely flowers, and all the children were grateful to Bobby and his gardening.

The summer term went on. There was to be a concert and a craftwork show at the end. Bobby wasn't in anything at the concert, except in the opening song, because he simply couldn't remember the words in any play or recitation for more than a day. He couldn't even sing in tune, so Miss Brown told him not to sing too loudly in the opening song, in case he put the others off.

Bobby was the only child who had nothing on show in the craftwork display. He had been trying to make something, like the others, but his work was so bad that Miss Brown said she was sorry, but she couldn't possibly show it.

The lady at the big house was to come to hear the concert and open the show. But on the day before the concert she fell ill and couldn't come. The children were sorry because they liked her. But she sent rather an exciting message. "I have asked a friend of mine to come instead," she said. "She is a duchess, so I hope you will welcome her nicely and thank her properly for coming."

"A duchess!" said the children. "Goodness, Miss Brown – we'll all have to be extra smart, and won't we have to present her with a bouquet – a really beautiful bunch of flowers?"

"Yes, we shall," said Miss Brown. "I must order some at once. Now – who shall give the flowers to her?"

The top girl of the class felt certain she would be chosen. The boy who happened to be games captain just then hoped he would be. Suzette, the smartest girl in the class, remembered her beautiful new dress, and thought she ought to be the one to curtsey and present the flowers.

But suddenly little Mary spoke up. "Miss Brown, I think Bobby ought to present the bouquet! Look at all the lovely flowers he's grown for us this term. He ought to have some reward and he's not doing anything special in the concert, and he's got nothing in the craftwork show. I do think he ought to present the flowers."

There was a moment's silence and then all the children – yes, even the top girl, the games captain and Suzette – shouted out loudly, "Yes! yes! That's fair. Let Bobby do it! Let Bobby give the flowers!"

What an honour for Bobby. He sat blushing in his seat, his eyes shining.

What would his mother say when she saw him going up to the Duchess and bowing and presenting the bouquet? Bobby was as glad for his mother as he was for himself.

It was all settled – except that Bobby insisted that he should bring the bouquet from his own garden. "This week I've got the loveliest carnations and roses you ever saw," he said. "Better than in any of the shops. Real beauties – and I'd love to give them to the Duchess."

So Bobby picked his carnations and roses, made them into a magnificent bouquet, and took them to school the next afternoon. All the mothers were there, and some of the fathers. It was a great day for the school and the parents. The pretty Duchess drove up in a black car. The children cheered. She smiled and went up on to the little platform to speak to the children.

And then, very proudly, Bobby went up on to the platform too, carrying the flowers he had grown himself. He looked neat and tidy, his hair was well brushed, his shoes shone, and his nails were clean. Miss Brown was proud of him.

Bobby bowed and presented the bouquet to the Duchess. His mother almost cried for joy. The Duchess took the flowers and exclaimed over them.

"How beautiful! I have never, never had such a wonderful bouquet before! Oh, thank you. What glorious roses and carnations!"

Little Mary couldn't stop herself from calling out, "Bobby grew them himself. He picked them out of his own garden for you!"

"Good gracious! What a clever boy you must be!" said the Duchess. "How proud your school must be of you!"

Bobby was as red as a beetroot. He almost burst for joy. He was at the bottom of the form and always had been and here he was being told he was clever by the Duchess herself – and he knew the school was proud of him!

So they were. They were proud of him and they liked him. As for his mother, how she beamed when all the other mothers crowded round her afterwards, and praised her Bobby!

Bobby is grown up now. He is the head of a very fine flower-growing firm and he takes all the prizes there are. It's surprising what you can do, even if you are at the bottom of the class!

Impy Plays
a Trick

Impy lived next door to Mister Frown. He was afraid of Mister Frown, who looked as cross as his name. Mister Frown had no time for imps. He thought they were a tiresome nuisance, and he said so, very loudly, whenever he saw Impy in the distance.

"Nasty little nuisances!" he said. "They never do any work. They are lazy, good-for-nothing creatures. Wait till I get hold of one!"

So, as you can guess, Impy kept well out of Mister Frown's way. The worst of it was that when Impy played with his ball in his garden, it would bounce over into Mister Frown's garden! And his kite would fly down there! And his arrows would dart straight into

Mister Frown's garden and stay there.

Impy didn't dare to go and get them. He didn't even dare to ask for them. He just peeped over the wall very sadly, and saw all his nice toys next door. He knew Mister Frown would never throw them back to him.

Mister Frown saw them there and he grinned to himself.

"Ho!" he said, "so that tiresome little Impy has lost some of his toys! Well, let him! I'm not going to throw them back – he can go without them. He won't dare to ask me for them."

But one day something else of Impy's went into Mister Frown's garden. Impy had done his washing, and had washed his best yellow coat, his new yellow scarf, and his yellow stockings. He had pegged them up on the line, and there they waved in the wind.

But Impy's pegs were not very good. They were old, and that day the wind blew very strongly indeed. You should have seen how those clothes pulled at the pegs! And it wasn't very long before the wind pulled the clothes right off the line and into Mister Frown's garden next door.

Impy was looking out of his window when it happened. He went quite pale when he saw what was happening. First his coat went – then the stockings and then the lovely yellow scarf! They all flapped quickly over the wall, and draped themselves neatly on the rosebushes next door.

"Look at that!" said Impy to himself. "Now what am I to do? All my balls are next door, and my fine red kite, and all my arrows belonging to my wooden bow, and now my best clothes have blown there. Whatever shall I do?"

Should he go and ask for them? No – he dared not do that. Should he wait till Mister Frown was out? No – for he might come back and catch him. That would be dreadful!

Poor little Impy. He sat and thought for a long while and then he grinned a little grin. He had thought of an idea but he didn't know if it would work or not.

He hunted for his long measuring-tape. Then he set out to the market. He knew that Mister Frown would be along that way to do his shopping very soon. And Impy had a plan to keep him away long enough for him to get the things he had lost.

Impy hummed a little tune, undid his long measuring-tape, and pretended to measure the wall and the pavement near a corner of the street. Nobody took any

notice of him. They thought he was a workman doing a job.

Presently along came Mister Frown, carrying his big shopping bag. He was surprised to see Impy with his measuring-tape.

"First time I've ever seen you working, Impy," he said. "Dear, dear, this is very strange!"

"I'm very busy," said Impy. "I've got to make notes of this corner of the street, and measure it carefully. The worst of it is that I've no one to hold the other end of the measure for me. So the tape keeps slipping."

"Well, I don't mind holding it for you," said Mister Frown, thinking that as long as Impy was at the other end of the tape he certainly couldn't slip home and take his clothes from the garden. "I'll hold one end."

"Oh, thank you, Mister Frown, how very kind you are!" said Impy. He held out one end of the tape to Mister Frown who took it.

"Now would you please hold it tightly while I pop round the corner with the other end of the tape?" asked Impy. "Keep a good pull on it, won't you, so that we get the length quite right. I have to measure from here to right round the corner."

Mister Frown held the end of the tape tightly. He saw Impy go round the corner. He felt someone at the other end, holding it tightly. He thought Impy was holding it just as tightly as he was.

But Impy wasn't! Impy had found Tickles the brownie round the corner and had beckoned to him.

"Here, Tickles! Would you be good

enough to hold the end of this tape for me while I go round the corner and hold the other end? I want to measure just here."

Tickles took the other end at once. Impy thanked him, slipped across the road, went down a side-turning, and ran home as fast as ever he could – leaving his measuring-tape carefully held by Mister Frown and Tickles. They couldn't see one another because they were each round a corner – and, dear me, they each thought that the other end of the tape was held by Impy!

Impy giggled as he ran home. He rushed into Mister Frown's garden and quickly found his balls, his kite, his arrows, and his clothes. He threw everything except his clothes over the wall, and then, carrying his yellow coat, stockings, and scarf he slipped out of Mister Frown's garden and into his own house. He locked the door and shut the windows.

He waited for Mister Frown to come home. What would he say? What was he doing now?

Well, Mister Frown was not a very patient man, and after he had held the tape for about four minutes he began to frown. Tickles, the brownie, thought that Impy was being a long time too, and he pulled impatiently on the tape.

Mister Frown felt the pull, and he pulled back.

"Hurry up!" yelled Mister Frown.

"Hurry up yourself!" Tickles yelled back.

Mister Frown tugged the tape crossly and Tickles almost fell over. He jerked his end roughly too, and Mister Frown fell over his shopping bag and hurt his knee.

"Stop it!" yelled Mister Frown angrily.

"Well, you stop it then!" shouted Tickles.

"I'll come and spank you!" roared Mister Frown, and letting go of his end of the tape he rushed round the corner, expecting to find Impy holding the other end. But to his great surprise he saw Tickles there!

"What are you holding that for?" he asked.

"Because Impy asked me to," said Tickles.

Mister Frown stared in amazement. "But he asked me as well!" he said. "I've been holding on all this time – and so have you too. Well, where is Impy?"

"I don't know," said Tickles crossly. "This is just one of his silly tricks, I suppose. Goodbye. I'm off!"

Mister Frown stared after him, thinking hard. A trick, was it? Ah – now he had it – Impy wanted to get home and take those clothes that had blown into the garden – and he had played this trick on Mister Frown so that he could keep him safely out of the way.

"Grrr!" Mister Frown growled like a dog and shot off down the street, quite forgetting his shopping bag. He ran all the way home, puffing and panting. As soon as he got into his back garden he saw that the balls, the kite, the arrows, and the clothes had all gone!

"Oh, the artful imp! Oh, the sly fellow!" cried Mister Frown in a rage, and he ran up the path to Impy's door.

He banged hard. No answer. He knocked again. Still no answer.

He went to the windows. They were shut and fastened. But when Mister Frown peeped into one, he saw Impy sitting indoors, dressed in his yellow clothes, grinning away for all he was worth.

"You played a trick on me, you wicked imp!" roared Mister Frown. "How dare you make me hold that tape when all you wanted was to get back home and take things out of my garden!"

Just then Mister Plod the policeman came by, and when he heard what Mister Frown said he went up to him.

"What's all this?" he said. "Has Impy been taking things out of your garden?"

"Yes," said Mister Frown. "He has."

"That's stealing," said Mister Plod. "What has he taken?"

"Four balls, six arrows, one kite, and a suit of yellow clothes!" yelled Impy, opening the window.

"You naughty little imp!" said the policeman. "Who did they belong to?"

"They belonged to me!" said Impy with a grin.

"Well, you can't steal things from yourself," said Mister Plod, shutting his notebook. "Mister Frown, don't be silly. Go home and behave yourself."

So Mister Frown went to his own house, red with rage – and Impy began to sing, "Oh, dear, what can the matter be?" at the top of his naughty little voice.

stay till you come out and kneel down to me and beg my pardon! Then you'll get a box on your ears and the kitten will get its tail pulled too."

Geoffrey yelled back at once, "You can wait for a year and I won't do that. Let me out."

"Shan't!" cried Tom. "The window is too tiny for you to squeeze through and the door's locked. Stay there till night if you want to."

Geoffrey heard his footsteps going back up the path. He went to the door and shook it. It was well and truly locked. Blow! He looked at the tiny window. He opened it but he knew he would never, never be able to squeeze through that!

"Blow Tom! He's a beast!" thought Geoffrey, stroking the frightened, wet kitten. He got out a hanky and began to dry the little thing.

Then a sudden thought struck him. He had to go out with his mother that afternoon to see his grandmother, who was ill. They were to catch the half-past three train. What ever would she do if he wasn't there to go with her? She would think something dreadful had happened to him! Then she wouldn't catch the train – and Granny would worry about their not coming to see her.

"Blow Tom!" he said again. "I simply must get out of this shed! Hey, Tom! Tom! TOM!"

He rattled the door again and soon Tom came up. "Ready to kneel down and apologise and have your ears boxed?" said Tom from outside the door.

"Tom, don't be an ass. I'm catching a train with my mother this afternoon to go and see my grandmother, who is ill," said Geoffrey. "I must go!"

"Not unless you do what I say," said Tom. "Well, call again if you change your mind."

And off he went once more, whistling. Geoffrey felt so angry that he nearly broke the door down! But it was strong and he couldn't budge it an inch.

He sat down on a box, panting. Paddy-Paws looked at him with big kitten-eyes. She wished she could help.

And then Geoffrey gave a little whistle and smiled. "Paddy-Paws, you can get us out of this! Do you remember your trick of taking messages? Well, take one now!"

He scribbled a note in a page of his notebook, tore it out, slipped a bit of string through one end and tied the note round the kitten's neck. Then he lifted her up to the window.

"Go to Mother," he said. "Find Mother for me. Hurry, little kitten!"

Paddy disappeared out of the window. She ran cautiously up the path, made for the wall and leaped on the top. She jumped down the other side and sped up to the house.

Geoffrey's mother was in her bedroom getting ready to go. Downstairs in the sitting-room was Geoffrey's father. He had come home unexpectedly, thinking that he too, would like to go and see his mother. The kitten saw him and ran to him. She jumped up on his knee.

He saw the note tied round her neck, and took it off in surprise. He read it.

Mother, Tom has locked me in the shed at the bottom of his garden. He put Paddy into the pond, that's why I went into his garden. I can't get out. Geoff.

"That boy!" said Geoffrey's father, angrily. He had no time for Tom – a rude, ill-mannered boy full of silly tricks. Putting a kitten into the pond – and then locking Geoffrey up for rescuing it. He wanted dealing with!

He went next door. Tom's father was there and the two men had a few words together. Geoffrey's father told him curtly that Tom had locked Geoffrey in his shed and he wanted him out quickly.

"Oh, it's just a joke, I expect," said Tom's father. "I'll come down the garden with you."

So down they went – and as they got near the shed they heard the two boys shouting at one another.

"Are you going to come out and kneel down to me and apologise and get your ears boxed? And I tell you I'm going to take that silly kitten and throw her over the wall!"

"You're a cowardly bully!" shouted back Geoffrey. "You might have drowned my kitten, putting her in the pond like that. I bet your father would be angry if he knew the things you do!"

"Pooh! What do I care for Dad?" shouted back Tom. "I do as I like. He thinks I'm the cat's whiskers! I don't take any notice of my dad!"

Well! His father could hardly believe his ears! As for Geoffrey's father, he smiled grimly. Perhaps Tom's father would now see that his boy wasn't all he thought him to be!

The two men came up to the startled

Tom. He was about to make a hurried explanation when his own father cut him short.

"Let Geoffrey out. How dare you do a thing like this? And I've got plenty to say to you about putting kittens into ponds. My word, I never thought to hear what I've just heard you say about me! So you don't take any notice of your dad, you say? Well, my boy, you're going to take so much notice of me that it will be a full-time job for you!"

Tom unlocked the door, beginning to shake at the knees. His father was usually easy-going, but when he got into one of his tremendous rages, all kinds of unpleasant things happened. Geoffrey appeared from the shed.

"Where's the kitten?" asked Tom's father.

"She went out of the window," said Geoffrey. He turned to his own father. "Thanks, Dad, for coming to get me out," he said.

Without another word he and his father went back home. Tom was left with his own father, looking very scared indeed. His father took him by one ear. It hurt.

"Now just come along with me and hear what is going to happen to you," he said, grimly. "So you do as you like, do you? Well, that's all coming to an end now. Come into the house, Tom."

Geoffrey was glad he wasn't Tom that afternoon. He made a fuss of the kitten and gave her some creamy milk as a reward for taking the note. Then he

hurriedly put on clean clothes and went to catch the train with his mother.

"Goodbye, cleverest kitten!" he said to Paddy-Paws. "I don't somehow think we shall ever have to be careful of Tom again!"

Poor Tom! He's very careful how he behaves now – and dear me, how he respects his father! That's just as it should be, of course. But what puzzles Tom is this: how did Geoffrey's father know that Geoffrey was locked up in that shed? Nobody has ever told Tom the answer – and I'm certainly not going to!

Good old Paddy-Paws. She's a cat now, but she's still just as clever as ever she was. She will take a message for you any day!

It Grew and
It Grew

Once little Fibs the pixie told his mother a story. He often didn't tell the truth, and it made her sad.

Fibs had been playing with his ball in the garden and it had landed on the rose-bed. He had gone to get it and had trodden all over the bed and broken some roses off.

"Oh, Fibs – did you do that?" cried his mother.

"No. It was Frisky the dog," said Fibs.

"Then he's very naughty," said his mother. "Go and find him and tie him up."

Fibs didn't want to do that. He liked Frisky. But he ran out and pretended to look for him. "Mother, he's frightened and he's gone into the next-door garden," he said, when he came back. That was another fib, of course. That first fib was certainly growing!

"Oh dear!" said his mother in dismay. "Dame Pitpat has hens, and if Frisky chases them she will be so cross. Go and ask her if she will let you go into her garden and catch him."

Fibs ran off. He went next door and pretended to ring the bell. Nobody came, of course, because he hadn't rung the bell. He ran back to his mother.

"Dame Pitpat is out," he said. "I rang and I rang, and nobody came. But never mind – Frisky ran out of her garden and he's gone down the road."

"Well, that's good," said his mother. "But I shall certainly tie him up when he comes in."

She went into the garden to hang up some clothes. Fibs heaved a sigh of relief. Perhaps now he needn't tell another fib.

Soon his mother came hurrying in. "Fibs, Fibs, where are you? There's a burglar in Dame Pitpat's house. There must be, because you said she was out. I distinctly saw someone at the upstairs window. You go and ask old Rappy to come along and find out!"

Fibs sighed. Oh dear, oh dear! It was all beginning again! He ran out to Mr Rappy's house, but he didn't knock at the door. He just stood there – then he went back again to his mother.

"Mr Rappy says he's got a very bad leg and he can't come. He says you must have been mistaken. There can't be a burglar in Dame Pitpat's house."

"How does *he* know?" cried his mother. "Well, then, I shall send you to Mr Plod the policeman. *Somebody* must come and get the burglar next door! Run, Fibs, run and get Mr Plod at once."

Fibs couldn't think what to do! He was standing there, wondering what to say, when his mother gave a loud cry. "Oh! There is Mr Plod! Look, by the front gate. Go and get him at once!"

Fibs went out slowly, hoping that Mr Plod would have gone by the time he reached the gate. His mother ran out crossly. "Why don't you hurry, Fibs? Mr Plod, Mr Plod! There's a robber in Dame Pitpat's house!"

Mr Plod turned in surprise. "Is there really, ma'am? Then I'll climb in at a window and catch him right away!"

And in no time at all there was Mr Plod climbing in at a window of Dame Pitpat's house! There was nobody downstairs so he went upstairs very quietly and walked into the bedroom.

Somebody screamed and sat up in bed! It was Dame Pitpat herself, having a

little rest. "Oh, what is it? Who is it? Why, it's Mr Plod! What do you want, Mr Plod?"

"Well, I was told there was a burglar in the house," said Mr Plod. "Little Fibs next door was sent to you with a message and he came back and said you were out, and then his mother saw somebody moving in the upstairs room, and . . ."

"Bless us all! I wasn't out!" said Dame Pitpat. "He couldn't have rung the bell or I'd have heard it. It was me that Fibs's mother saw upstairs. Please go away, Mr Plod, and leave me in peace."

Mr Plod went down and told Fibs's mother and she was really very puzzled. She was even more puzzled when she saw Mr Rappy coming out of his house with his stick under his arm, walking quickly to catch the bus.

"Why, Mr Rappy! When Fibs asked you for help just now, you told him you couldn't come because you had a very bad leg!" cried Fibs's mother, looking most amazed.

"Nonsense!" said Mr Rappy. "He never

came to ask me anything at all. Just one of his tales!" He rapped with his stick on the fence. "He wants a taste of this – then he wouldn't tell so many stories!"

"Fibs! You didn't go to Mr Rappy – and I don't believe you went to Dame Pitpat's either!" said his mother, shocked. "And I don't suppose Frisky was in her garden. Where *is* he then? Frisky, Frisky!"

A loud barking came from upstairs. Fibs's mother ran up and opened a door. Inside the room was Frisky, wagging his tail.

"Why, he's been here all the time," said Fibs's mother. "He's been asleep on his rug. He *couldn't* have run over the rose-bed and broken the roses. Then who did, Fibs? Answer me that!"

She went out to the rose-bed – and there she saw the footprints quite clearly. They were Fibs's, of course.

"You horrid, mean, little pixie!" she cried. "Blaming poor Frisky – telling me he had run away next door – and saying that Dame Pitpat was out and Mr Rappy had a bad leg. Don't you know that one fib leads to another and always brings trouble in the end? Well, trouble is coming to you, Fibs!"

Poor Fibs! His mother told the truth – it was ages before he was allowed out to play again. It's strange how one fib leads to another, isn't it? Fibs knows that now and he'll never forget it!

Down
the Rabbit-Hole

Jiffy was a little pixie. He was servant to six of the ugliest goblins you could imagine – and how he worked for them!

He lit the fires and made the beds, he scrubbed the floor and cooked the dinner, he cleaned the windows and washed the clothes – well, really, there was no end to the things he did for the six goblins.

One day he had a cold. Dear me, it was really a terrible cold. He sneezed and coughed and he didn't feel at all well.

"Please," he said to the least ugly goblin, "may I stay in bed today? I really don't think I can do any work."

"What! And on marketing day too!" shouted the goblin. "Whoever heard of such a thing? Certainly not!"

So poor Jiffy had to take his basket

and go trudging over Bumble-bee Common.

Just as he passed a big rabbit-hole he stopped. He was going to sneeze. He knew he was. It was coming – it was coming – it was – *a-tishoo*! It was coming again – A-TISHOO! Oh dear! Oh dear!

Poor little Jiffy. He sneezed his hat off. He sneezed his ears all crooked. He dropped his basket. He sat down by the rabbit-hole and began to cry because he felt so miserable.

Mrs Sandy Rabbit heard him. She popped her woffly nose out of the nearby hole and looked all round to see who had been sneezing. She was a big, fat, motherly rabbit and she stared in surprise at Jiffy.

"You ought to be in bed," she said.

"They won't let me," said Jiffy.

"Who won't?" asked Mrs Sandy Rabbit.

"The goblins I work for," said Jiffy.

"What! Those ugly, double-jointed, snaggle-toothed creatures!" cried Mrs Sandy Rabbit. "Never you mind about them! You come along down my hole and I'll put you to bed in Fluffy's cot – he's just grown out of it – and you can stay there till you're better."

"But – but – but . . ." began Jiffy.

"There's no time for buts," said Mrs Sandy Rabbit. "Come along."

She shooed him down her warm dark hole to the bottom. Very far down there was a big room. In it were some beds, tables, and chairs, and a bright little lamp. Mrs Sandy Rabbit undressed Jiffy, put him into pyjamas of Fluffy's and

popped him into bed. Then she made him some hot cocoa.

How warm he was! How comfortable! How delicious the cocoa was! Nobody had ever made him cocoa to drink before. No one had ever tucked him up before – and what was this! Mrs Sandy Rabbit was tucking a hot-water bottle at his feet. Oh, how perfectly lovely!

Suddenly he sat up in alarm.

"Mrs Sandy Rabbit! Mrs Sandy Rabbit! Suppose those goblins come for me?"

"Don't you worry," said Mrs Sandy Rabbit. "*I'll* tell them a few things!"

Well, of course the goblins were furious when they found out that Jiffy hadn't come home. There was no lunch for them – no tea. The floor was dirty. Their suits were not ironed. Dear, dear, dear!

"We'll go out and look for him, and what a telling-off he'll get when we drag him back!" said the goblins. So off they went – and very soon they found his market basket on the ground outside Mrs Sandy Rabbit's hole. Oho! So he was down there, was he!

Down the hole went the six goblins
and came to Mrs Sandy Rabbit's door.
They knocked: *Blim-blam, blim-blam*.

Mrs Sandy Rabbit opened the door and
scowled at them. She pretended that she
thought they were bringing the washing
back.

"I hope you've got the clothes clean
this week!" she grumbled. "Where's the
basket? Don't tell me you've forgotten
it! And dear me, did it take six of you to
bring it this week?"

"We're not the washing," said the goblins.

"Oh, then you must be the men come to mend the clock," said Mrs Sandy Rabbit. "Which of you mended it last time? – because whoever it was lost the key. Just wait till I know which of you it was – I'll pull his nasty little goblin nose for him!"

The goblins began to feel rather afraid of this fierce rabbit. They spoke quite humbly and politely to her.

"We haven't come to mend the clock. We've come to ask you which way to go to find Jiffy, our servant. He seems to have run away."

"And I don't wonder," said Mrs Sandy Rabbit. "Well, I'll tell you which way to go and what to do – and though I don't say you'll find Jiffy if you do what I tell you, you never know!"

"Oh, we'll do exactly what you tell us, Mrs Sandy Rabbit," said the goblins eagerly. "Exactly."

"Well, go down the passage to the right over there," said Mrs Sandy Rabbit, pointing, "and you'll come to a big tree-root. Scrape as hard as you can where you see the root, and you'll come out into a big room of some sort. I don't say you'll find Jiffy there – but you'll find some-one all right."

"Thank you," said the goblins and ran off to the right. They came to the tree-root and started to dig and scrape for all they were worth.

Now, although they didn't know it, a fox and his wife had their den just there, with six young cubs. All the rabbits kept away from that particular passage because they knew that on the other side of the wall of earth lived a family of foxes, but the goblins thought that Jiffy was hiding there!

So they scrabbled and scraped and dug for all they were worth. The foxes pricked up their ears and waited. Was this rabbits? If so, what a nice dinner!

Suddenly the goblins broke down the last bit of earth and squeezed through into the foxhole. The foxes sprang on them – and found them to be goblins and not rabbits!

"Let us go, let us go!" squealed the goblins, frightened. "Where's Jiffy?"

"I don't know who, where, or what Jiffy is!" said the fox fiercely. "What I want to know is – how dare you make a hole into our den like that! Do you want to be eaten?"

"No," squeaked the goblins, terrified.

"What shall we do with them?" the fox asked his wife.

"Well," she said, looking at the goblins. "There are six goblins – and we have six cubs. That would be a servant for each of them, to brush their coats, take them out for walks, and look after them properly. They can either be eaten – or be our servants – whichever they please."

Well you can easily guess which the goblins chose – and after that they acted as nursemaids to the six spoilt young foxes, who nipped the goblins' ears whenever they were bad-tempered, which was very often!

Jiffy had a lovely time with Mrs Sandy Rabbit in her cosy little home. His cold soon got better, and he thought he had better go home again – but when he got to the cottage it was empty! There were no goblins there at all!

"Oooh!" said Jiffy, in excitement. "The goblins have gone! I'll get Mrs Sandy Rabbit to come and live here with all her family – and I'll look after them and be as happy as the day is long!"

So Mrs Sandy Rabbit and all her fluffy family moved into the goblins' cottage, which was really much more convenient than the dark hole. And there they all lived happily together until the day when the foxes set the goblins free once more.

And then, of course, they all came wandering home again to their cottage! Oh dear!

But Mrs Sandy Rabbit saw them coming up the path. She opened the door, crossed her arms and said, "And what do you want *this* time? If you're the baker, you're late, and I'll chase away the lot of you! If you are the new gardeners, you won't do, so go before I set the dog on you – and if you're nursemaids out of a job, I can tell you of a nice fox family who have twelve fox cubs and . . ."

"Ooooh!" squealed the goblins in fright, and fled away as fast as ever they could. Fox cubs! Never again! They would go off to the moon rather than look after bad-tempered foxes!

So off to the moon they went. There are no foxes there so they are happy. As for Jiffy, he couldn't be happier. You should see him wheeling out the youngest baby rabbits! They all love him and he loves them – and what could be nicer than that?

Sly-One
Buys His Apples

There was once a rascally brownie called Sly-One, who bought fine red apples at a penny each, and sold them at a penny each, too. Now you might think that that was a silly thing to do, because he wouldn't make any money for himself – but he did! He became very rich, and all the brownies thought that there really must be some magic about his buying and selling.

Now one day I happened to be near when Sly-One was buying his apples from the Apple-Woman who lives down Cuckoo Lane. He was counting them out from a tub and putting them on to his barrow, and I could see and hear plainly what he was doing. He wanted fifty apples, and as I stood there and watched him, he began counting them:

"One, two, three, four, five, six, seven, eight, nine," he counted aloud. "My, Apple-Woman, there's a fine red apple for you! It's so red it reminds me of the cheeks of that little girl who lives down Cradle Valley. She's a bonny little thing, and only five years old, too! Yes, only five! Five, six, seven, eight, nine, ten, eleven, twelve, thirteen, fourteen, fifteen – hey! Is that one of your hens got loose? Look, there it is running over the road. How many hens have you got, Apple-

Woman? Twelve! My, that's a fine lot, isn't it? Twelve! Twelve, thirteen, fourteen, fifteen, sixteen, seventeen, eighteen, nineteen, twenty, twenty-one, twenty-two – oh, excuse me, I'm going to sneeze!"

Sly-One took out his handkerchief and did a most tremendous sneeze.

"A-tishoo! A-TISHOO!" he sneezed. Then he put his handkerchief away.

"The other day I sneezed twenty times running!" he told the Apple-Woman. "Twenty! Just think of it. Twenty, twenty-one, twenty-two, twenty-three, twenty-four, twenty-five, twenty-six, twenty-seven, and twenty-eight, twenty-nine, thirty, thirty-one, thirty-two, thirty-three, thirty-four – that's the number of your little house, Apple-Woman, isn't it? Now, I live at number thirty-one. Thirty-one, thirty-two, and thirty-three, thirty-four, thirty-five, thirty-six, thirty-seven, thirty-eight, and thirty-nine, forty, forty-one, forty-two, forty-three, forty-four, forty-five, forty-six – that reminds me, Apple-Woman,

there were forty-six rooks in my garden yesterday – what do you think of that? And the day before that there were forty-two! Forty-two! Forty-three, forty-four, forty-five ..."

Now I wonder if you can see the trick that Sly-One was playing on the poor old Apple-Woman. She listened to him talking, and saw him taking out the apples one by one, and she didn't know that although he seemed to be counting them very carefully, he was taking far more than he should.

He went on counting. "Forty-five, forty-six, forty-seven, forty-eight – that's how old I am, Apple-Woman – forty-eight last birthday. My, how the time does fly, doesn't it? It seems only the other day that I was forty-one, yes, surely, it does. Forty-one! Forty-two, forty-three, forty-four, forty-five, forty-six, forty-seven, forty-eight, forty-nine – do you know, Apple-Woman, I have got forty-nine buttons on my new coat – no, I'm wrong. I lost one yesterday, so there's only forty-eight now. Yes, forty-eight. Forty-eight, forty-nine, fifty!"

He put the last apple on his barrow, and paid the Apple-Woman fifty pennies for them. Then he politely said good morning, raised his pointed cap, and wheeled his barrow away. But do you know how many apples the old rascal had on his brightly-painted barrow?

He had eighty-three, for which he had only paid fifty pennies. The Apple-Woman thought that her apple-tub looked rather empty, but as she had heard the brownie counting the apples, she thought it must be all right.

Now not long after that I happened to pass by Sly-One's cottage, and I saw him selling fifty apples to a customer who had bought a bag in which to take them

away. I stopped and listened to him selling them, and this is how he sold them.

"You want fifty apples, Pippitty," he said. "Very well, I have some fine ones here. I'll count them out for you, if you'll hold out your bag. Now then – one, two, three, four, five, six, seven, eight – how's your sister, Pippitty? She wasn't at all well when I saw her last. Oh, I'm glad she's better. Let me see, how many sisters and brothers have you got? Fifteen! My, that's a great number! Fifteen! Fifteen, sixteen, seventeen, eighteen, nineteen, twenty, twenty-one – by the way, did you know that the Queen is going to have twenty-one fiddlers at the next dance? Yes, she is, really. There was a talk about having thirty-one! Fancy that! Thirty-one!"

Sly-One popped the apples into the bag as he talked, and his customer listened to him.

"Thirty-one, thirty-two, thirty-three, thirty-four – have you heard that poor old Raggedy the gnome has been turned out of the cottage he's lived in for thirty-four years?" asked Sly-One. "Yes, thirty-four years he's lived there, and he told me, poor old chap, that he had hoped to live there for forty-eight years. But he won't now. Forty-eight, forty-nine, fifty. There, that's the lot. Have you brought your fifty pennies with you?"

Pippitty had, and he handed them over to Sly-One. Then he went off with his bag, thinking that he had got fifty fine red apples in it. Hadn't he heard Sly-One count them?

But alas for poor old Pippitty! He had only got twenty-two!

And it's no wonder that Sly-One gets rich, is it? For he had got back the fifty pennies he had spent that morning, and on his barrow he still had sixty-one apples left to sell!

But that sort of thing really can't be allowed, so tomorrow I am going to the Apple-Woman, and I shall ask her if she will let me count her apples out to Sly-One when he comes to buy them. I shall play his own trick on him – and I do wonder what he'll do, don't you?

The Little
Sewing Machine

Dorothy had a little sewing machine for her birthday. She was so pleased with it, for it really could sew. It had a little wheel, and when she turned the handle of the wheel, with her hand, the needle went up and down very fast indeed and stitched the cloth that Dorothy wanted to make into coats and dresses for her dolls.

It was only a toy sewing machine, but Dorothy liked it very much. She could not sew so beautifully with it as her mother could sew with her big sewing machine, but still, it was quite big enough to make all sorts of clothes for her toys.

The toys sat round her each day and watched her sewing with her little machine. Teddy was delighted because he had a new red coat. Angeline, the big doll, was pleased because she had a new petticoat with lace all round the edge. The yellow rabbit wore a new scarf and cap to match, both made by the little sewing machine.

At night, when Dorothy was in bed, the toys used to talk to the pixies who lived outside the window, in the snowdrop-bed. The teddy bear showed them his coat, the doll showed her fine petticoat, and the little yellow rabbit took his cap and scarf off to let the pixies see how beautiful they were.

"Who makes your clothes for you?" asked the teddy bear.

"Oh, the Fairy Silvertoes makes all our things," said one of the pixies. "She is very clever, you know. All the spiders in the garden give her thread, and she dyes it in the loveliest colours. Then she sews petals and leaves together and makes all our clothes. I really don't know what we would do without her."

"Does she make your party clothes, too?" asked the yellow rabbit.

"Of course!" said the pixies. "There is a very grand party on full-moon night this month, and Fairy Silvertoes has promised to make all our clothes for us. We can't go in these old things – we've had them ever since the autumn! We want new ones now."

"I'm going to have mine made of snowdrop petals with a hat to match," said another pixie.

"And I'm having mine made of brown oak-leaves, trimmed with bright green moss," said another.

"Goodness, Fairy Silvertoes will be very busy!" said the doll.

Now one night the pixies came to talk

to the toys, and they had very long faces indeed.

"What's the matter?" asked the teddy bear, in surprise.

"Something awful has happened!" said the pixies. "Our Fairy Silvertoes has cut her hand very badly, and she can't use it for sewing until it's better."

"Dear, dear, we're sorry to hear that!" said the teddy bear.

"You see, she was making our party clothes, and she hadn't really very much to do to finish them," said a tall pixie, dolefully. "It will be dreadful if her hand doesn't get better very soon because some of us may not have our dresses ready and won't be able to go to the party!"

"That would be dreadful!" said the yellow rabbit, who loved parties and thought it was terrible to have to miss one.

"Wouldn't it be disappointing!" said the pixies, all together.

Then the teddy bear had a splendid idea. It was so splendid that he could hardly speak quickly enough to tell the others.

"I say, I say!" he shouted. "I know! Let's lend Fairy Silvertoes the little toy sewing machine! Then she can make all the clothes as fast as can be, and all the pixies will be able to go to the party!"

Everyone shouted in excitement. It really was a marvellous idea.

"Yes, yes!" cried the pixies. "That's what we'll do. We'll take it back with us tonight, and show Silvertoes how to use it."

"Wait a minute," said the big doll suddenly. "Ought we to lend it without asking Dorothy? After all, it doesn't belong to us. Suppose Fairy Silvertoes had an accident with it and broke it? Whatever would Dorothy say? She would be very angry with us for lending it without asking her."

"Well, let's ask her, then!" said the teddy bear.

"But she's asleep," said the doll.

"We can wake her, can't we?" said the yellow rabbit impatiently. "Come on. We'll all go and wake her."

So the big doll, the yellow rabbit, and the teddy bear ran out of the playroom and pushed open the door of Dorothy's bedroom. There was a little nightlight glowing in the room and they could see that Dorothy was fast asleep.

"Wake up, Dorothy, wake up!" said the teddy bear, and he patted the little girl's hand gently. But she didn't wake up. Then the big doll scrambled up on the bed and tapped Dorothy on the cheek.

"Do wake up, Dorothy," she said. "We want to ask you something."

Then Dorothy really did wake up and sat up in bed in surprise. She saw the doll, the rabbit, and the teddy bear, and at first she thought she must still be dreaming.

"Goodness!" she said. "What are you doing at this time of night, toys?"

"We've come to ask you something," said the teddy bear. "Listen."

Then he told Dorothy all about Fairy Silvertoes and her accident.

"And now we wonder if you'll be kind enough to lend your sewing machine to her," he said. "You see, she could easily work that without hurting her cut hand, and then she could finish all the dresses in time!"

"Of course I'll lend it to her!" said Dorothy, really most excited. "Why, I'd

love to! But, toys, do you think the pixies would let me see Silvertoes using my machine? Oh, do ask them if I can! I could put on my dressing-gown and come."

The teddy bear ran off to ask the pixies. They said yes, certainly, but the next night would be best, because by that time they would have been able to explain to Fairy Silvertoes how to work the machine and she wouldn't be nervous if Dorothy came to watch.

"How perfectly lovely!" said Dorothy, sitting up in bed, squeezing her arms round her knees. "All right, toys, you can let the pixies have my sewing machine. But don't forget I'm coming to watch tomorrow night!"

The toys ran off. The pixies took the little sewing machine and carried it carefully down the garden to the thick holly bush. Fairy Silvertoes had a cosy house underneath it. They called her and she came to the door, her cut hand resting in a sling.

She was delighted when she saw the sewing machine. The pixies showed her exactly how to work it and she found that she could easily turn the wheel without hurting her hand.

"Oh, now I'll be able to make all your

dresses in plenty of time!" she cried. "You'll all go to the party now!"

The next night Dorothy could hardly lie still in bed. She so badly wanted to get up and go to watch Silvertoes, but she had to wait until the house was quiet and midnight had struck by the hall clock downstairs. Then the toys came alive and went to fetch her. She slipped out of bed, put on her dressing-gown, and went with them to the playroom. She climbed out of the window, slid down the pear tree outside, and ran down to the holly tree with the toys. The pixies were there waiting for her.

As she went near the tree she heard the whirr of her little sewing machine, and knew that Fairy Silvertoes was hard at work.

"We must make you a little smaller or you won't be able to get into Silvertoes' house," said one of the pixies. He touched her with his wand and she at once became about half her size. It was a very strange feeling. Then she saw Silvertoes' little house and cried out in delight. She went in and found the fairy hard at work with her machine, sewing the most dainty coats and tunics that Dorothy had ever seen.

"Let me help you!" said Dorothy, and the two of them worked the machine together, and held the cloth straight as the needle drew the thread through it. It was great fun.

"I shall be able to finish all these party dresses tonight," said Silvertoes happily. "Everyone will be so pleased. It's very good of you to lend me this lovely sewing machine, Dorothy. What can I do for you in return?"

"I suppose you couldn't make me a party dress for my smallest doll, could you?" asked Dorothy. "I have the dearest little doll with curly yellow hair and blue eyes, and I always take her out to tea with me when I go to see my friends. It would be lovely to have a fairy dress for her."

Well, Silvertoes made one! You should just see it! It was made of daffodil frills, trimmed with dewdrop beads, and suited the little doll perfectly.

Dorothy came to tea with me yesterday and brought the doll all dressed up in her fairy dress, so that's how I heard this story. Wouldn't you like to see the dress too? Well, just ask Dorothy to tea and you'll see it on her doll!

The Empty Doll's-House

Sally had a lovely little doll's-house for Christmas. She looked at it standing there at the foot of her bed. It had a little blue front door with a tiny knocker that really knocked, and it had four small windows, with tiny lace curtains at each one!

"Oh, it's lovely!" said Sally. "Won't my little Belinda Jane love to live there! She is just the right size."

But when she opened the front of the doll's-house, Sally got a shock. It was empty. There was no furniture at all!

She was disappointed. A doll's-house can't be played with unless it has furniture inside, and Sally badly wanted to play with it.

Also, Belinda Jane couldn't possibly live there if it was empty. She must at least have a bed to sleep in, a chair to sit on, and a table to have meals on.

She showed the house to Belinda Jane. Belinda looked sad when she saw that it was empty.

"Never mind. I'll save up my money and buy some furniture," said Sally. "Maybe I'll get some money today as a Christmas present."

But she didn't. All her aunts and uncles gave her toys and books for Christmas, and nobody gave her any money at all.

It was Granny who had given her the dear little doll's-house. When she came to have Christmas dinner with Sally's family she spoke to Sally about the house.

"I didn't put any furniture in it, dear," she said, "because I thought you would find it more fun to buy some yourself and furnish it bit by bit."

"Yes. It will be fun to do that," said Sally. "Only it will take such a long time, Granny, because I spent all my money on Christmas presents, and I only get fifty pence a week, you know."

When Sally got her first fifty pence
she went to the toyshop and looked at
the doll's-house furniture there. She saw
a cardboard box, and in it was a dear
little bed that would just fit Belinda Jane,
two chairs, a table and a wardrobe! Think
of that!

But, oh dear, it cost three pounds, and
there was nothing at all that just one
fifty pence would buy! Sally ran home
almost in tears!

"Now, don't be a baby," said her
mother. Everything comes to those who
wait patiently. Don't get cross and upset
if you can't have what you want right
away. It will come!"

Sally was not a very patient person,

and she hated waiting for things she badly wanted. But she always believed what her mother said, so she went up to her room and told Belinda Jane they must both be patient, and maybe they would get the furniture somehow in the end.

Sally was excited next day because she was going to a party and there was to be a Christmas tree. It was sure to be a nice big one, with a present for everyone. And there would be games and balloons and crackers and ice cream. Lovely!

She went to the party in her best blue party dress.

"Hello, Sally!" called Elaine, dashing up to her. "There's going to be a prize for every game, did you know? And it's to be money! I do hope I win a prize, because it's Mummy's birthday next week and I want to buy her some flowers."

Sally was pleased to hear about the prizes too. If only she could win some of the money! Then she would be able to buy some furniture for Belinda Jane.

They played musical chairs – but Sally

didn't win because a rough little boy pushed her out of her chair, and she didn't like to push back.

They played hunt the thimble, but somehow Sally never could find the thimble first! And when they played spin the platter she couldn't get there before the little spinning plate had fallen over flat! So she didn't win any prizes at all.

"Now, I mustn't get cross or upset," she said to herself. "I mustn't. I must be patient. But I've missed my chance. What a pity!"

After tea the children were taken into another room – and there was the Christmas tree, reaching to the ceiling, hung with presents from top to bottom. Just about in the middle of the tree there hung a cardboard box – just like the cardboard box of furniture that Sally had seen in the toyshop! Her heart jumped for joy. Now surely her patience would have its reward – surely she would get that lovely box of doll's-house furniture!

She could hardly wait for the presents to be given out. She had good manners, so she didn't like to ask for the box of furniture. She just stood near by, hoping it would be hers.

But to her very great disappointment, it wasn't given to her! She was handed a box with tiny motor-cars in it instead. Sally could have cried! She said "Thank you" and went away to a corner, trying not to feel upset.

"I wanted to win a prize and I didn't. And I wanted to have the furniture off the tree and I didn't," she thought. "What's the good of being patient? I don't get what I want, however good and patient I am. I feel like shouting and stamping!"

But she didn't shout or stamp, of course, because she knew better. She just sat and looked at the little motor-cars, and didn't like them a bit.

A small girl called Josie came up to her. She had the box of furniture in her hand. She sat down beside Sally and looked at the tiny motor-cars.

"Oh, aren't they lovely?" she said. "I do like them so much. I got this doll's-house furniture, look. Isn't it silly?"

"Well, I think it's lovely," said Sally. "How can you think it's silly?"

"It's silly for me, because I haven't got a doll's-house," said Josie. "But I *have* got a toy garage! I had it for Christmas. It's only got one car in, and I do want some more. That's why I like your present and hate mine!"

"Well, I was given a doll's-house for Christmas without any furniture – and I haven't got a garage!" said Sally, her face very bright. "Can't you give me the furniture and I'll give you the motor-cars? We could ask Elaine's mother, and see if she minds. She was the one who bought all the presents for us."

They found Elaine's mother, and asked her. She smiled at them. "Of course you can change your presents if you want to," she said. "I think it would be most sensible of you. I would have given you the furniture, Sally, and you the cars, Josie, if I'd known about the doll's-house and the garage."

The little girls were so pleased. Josie took her cars home to put in her garage and Sally raced home with her doll's-house furniture. It went into the doll's-house and looked most beautiful!

"There you are, Belinda Jane," said Sally to her smallest doll. "Now you can move in. You've got a bed to sleep in, chairs to sit on, a wardrobe for your clothes and a table to have meals on. And I'll buy you a little cooker as soon as I can."

Belinda Jane was pleased. She looked sweet sitting on one of the chairs, and even sweeter tucked up in the little bed.

Mother came to look. Sally gave her a hug. "Mummy, you were right about waiting patiently. I kept on being disappointed, but I wouldn't get cross or upset – and then suddenly the furniture just came to me. Wasn't it lucky?"

"It was," said her mother. "Now, tomorrow I'll give you some old bits and pieces and you can make carpets for Belinda Jane. She will like that."

You should see Sally's doll's-house now. She saved up her money and bought a little lamp, a cooker, another bed, a cupboard for the kitchen, two more chairs and a bookcase. I really wouldn't mind living in that doll's-house myself!

The Pig with
a Straight Tail

There was once a pig whose tail was as straight as a poker. This worried him very much, because all the tails belonging to his brothers and sisters were very curly indeed.

"Ha!" said his little fat sisters. "Look at Grunts! Whoever saw a pig with a straight tail before?"

"Ho!" said his big brothers. "Look at Grunts! Whoever saw a pig without a kink in his tail before?"

Poor Grunts was very much upset about it.

"I really must get my tail curly somehow," he thought to himself. "Now what can I do?"

He thought a little while and then he trotted off to old Dame Criss-Cross.

"Sometimes her hair is quite straight and sometimes it is curly," he said to himself. "I wonder what she does to it. I will ask her."

So he knocked on her little front door with his trotter. Dame Criss-Cross opened it, and was most surprised to see Grunts there.

"What do you want?" she asked.

"I want to know how to curl my tail," said Grunts. "I know you curl your hair, so I thought perhaps you could tell me."

Dame Criss-Cross laughed till the tears

came into her eyes. Then she went into her bedroom and fetched a great big curling-pin, the biggest she had got.

"Here you are, Grunts," she said. "Let me put your tail into this curling-pin and it will curl beautifully."

She rolled Grunts's tail up in the pin, and, oh dear, it did hurt! Grunts groaned loudly, but he so badly wanted a curly tail that he put up with the pain like a hero.

Off he went back to the pigsty, and, dear me, how all the big pigs and little pigs roared with laughter to see Grunts with his tail done up in a large curling-pin.

Next morning Grunts ran off to Dame Criss-Cross again, and she undid it for him. Oh, what a fine curly tail he had! It twisted itself up like a spring, and Grunts was terribly proud of it. He stood with his back to all the other pigs whenever he could, and they admired his tail very much, for it was even curlier than theirs.

But then a dreadful thing happened. It began to rain. Grunts took no notice, for he didn't mind the rain at all; but his beautiful curly tail got wet and all the curl came out!

"Your tail's straight! Your tail's straight!" cried all the pigs, crowding round him. Grunts looked over his back, and, sure enough, his tail was as straight as a poker again.

"Oh, bother!" said Grunts, in dismay. "It's no good putting it into curlers, that's quite plain. Now what shall I do?"

"Go to Tips the pixie and get her to put a curly spell in your tail," said the biggest pig of all.

So off went Grunts to Tips's little cottage and banged at her door with his trotter.

"What do you want, Grunts?" she asked.

"Can you put a curly spell in my tail?" asked Grunts. "It's so dreadfully straight."

"Well, I'll try," said Tips, doubtfully. "But I don't know if I've a spell that is strong enough. Your tail is really too terribly straight!"

She fetched a blue bowl, and put into it six strange things – a golden feather with a blue tip, a spider's web heavy with dew, a centre of a young daisy, the whisker of a gooseberry, a hair from a red squirrel, and a spoonful of moonlight taken from a puddle. Then she stirred the mixture up together, singing a little magic song.

"Now turn round and put your tail in the bowl," said Tips. "The spell will make it curly."

So Grunts turned round and put his straight little tail into the blue bowl. The pixie stirred the mixture all over it, and gradually it became curlier and curlier. Tips was delighted.

"It has made it curly," she said. "But I don't know how long it will stay like that, Grunts."

"Will rain hurt it?" asked the little pig.

"No," said Tips, "I don't think so. My, you do look fine!"

Off went Grunts back to the pigsty, and all the pigs admired him very much. But – wasn't it a pity? – the sun came out and shone down so hotly that poor Grunts's tail began to go limp again! And soon it was just as straight as ever. The sun had melted away the curly spell.

"Well, I'm sure I don't know *what* to do!" said Grunts in dismay.

"What's the matter?" asked an old witch who happened to be passing by. So Grunts told her his trouble.

"Oh, you want a very, very strong spell," said the witch. "You had better come to me – I can give you one that will make your tail very curly indeed."

Now, the wicked old witch didn't mean to do anything of the sort. She just wanted to get hold of Grunts and make him into bacon, for he was a very fat little pig. But Grunts didn't know she was wicked, and he felt most excited.

"Come to me at midnight tonight," said the witch. "My cottage is in the middle of Hawthorn Wood."

So that night, at just about half past eleven, Grunts set out. It was very dark, and when he got into the wood it was darker still. Grunts began to feel frightened.

Then something made him jump terribly.

"Too-whit, too-whit!" said a loud voice.

"Too-whoo, too-whoo!" said another. Grunts gave a squeal and began to run.

He didn't know it was only a pair of owls calling to one another. Then something else gave him a fright. The moon rose and looked at him through the trees.

"Ooh!" squealed the little pig. "What is it? It's a giant's face looking at me!"

He stumbled on through the wood, quite losing his way. Suddenly he heard two voices nearby, and against the light of the moon he saw two witches.

"Have you seen a little fat pig?" asked one.

"No," said the other. "Why?"

"Oh, one was coming to me to get his tail made curly!" said the first one, with a laugh. "Silly little pig! He didn't know I was going to catch him and make him into bacon!"

Grunts crouched down in the bushes, and stayed quite still until the witches had gone away. All his bristles stood up on his back with fright, his tail curled up with fear, and he shivered like a jelly.

"What an escape I've had!" he thought. "Ooh, that wicked old witch. I'll go straight home as soon as it's dawn."

So when day came he looked around him, found the right path, and scampered home as fast as he could. Wasn't he glad to see the pigsty. But what a surprise he had when he got there!

"Oh, your tail is lovely and curly!" cried all his brothers and sisters. "Did the old witch put a spell on it?"

"No," said Grunts, in surprise, looking at his curly tail in delight. "Now whatever made it go like that? Why, I was almost frightened out of my life!"

"It was the fright that made your tail

curl!" said an old pig, wisely. "That's what it was! Didn't you feel something funny about it last night?"

"Now I come to think of it, I did," said the little pig. "Oh, my, what a funny thing! I escaped the old witch, got a terrible fright, and a curly tail! I wonder if it will last."

Day after day Grunts looked at his tail – and so far it is still as curly as ever. He is so pleased about it, of course!

The Grand
Birthday Cake

Helen lived in a little house that stood next to a very big one. In the big house lived three children, and they had fine games together. Helen used to watch them from her bedroom window and wish that she could play too.

Helen had no brothers or sisters. She lived alone with her grandmother, and because they were very poor she had hardly any friends. Her granny did not like her to ask other children to tea because it meant buying cakes and she said she couldn't afford it. So Helen played alone and it was very dull indeed.

She loved watching the three children next door. They were so happy, so kind to one another, and they had so many toys! There was a seesaw in the garden, a swing and a little swimming-pool – so you can guess they had plenty to do ! When Helen saw the three children looking at her, she always looked the other way. She blushed because her dress was darned and mended, and her shoes so old. She felt sure that the three children would laugh at her if she gave them a chance. Their clothes were so lovely, and they always looked so pretty and clean.

One day Helen heard the children talking about a birthday party. It was for Kitty, the youngest little girl. She was going to be five, and was to have a very grand birthday indeed.

"You were ill on your birthday last year, Kitty," said Mary, the eldest girl. "So this year we are going to give you a perfectly marvellous party to make up for last year!"

"Ooh!" said Kitty, in delight. "How lovely!"

"You're going to have a great big birthday cake with five fairies on it, each one holding a candle for you," said

Gillian, the other girl. "And after tea
there will be a conjuror doing tricks! And
there is to be a bran-tub with a present
for everyone in it – you too, Kitty!"

"Ooh!" said little Kitty, again, her face
red with delight.

Helen could hear everything that was
said. How she wished she could go to a
party like that! Fancy – a birthday cake
with five fairies on it holding candles!
And a conjuror! And a bran-tub with
presents for everyone!

Saturday was the day of the party, when Kitty was five. Helen saw the postman go that morning with heaps of brown paper parcels and cards, and she guessed they were for lucky Kitty.

"I wish I could see that birthday cake with fairies on," she thought longingly. "I expect they will be made of sugar and they will be lovely. I wonder if I could peep in at the window and see it."

Kitty had one present she loved very much – and that was a brown and white spaniel puppy! Her father gave it to her and she shrieked with delight.

"I shall put a ribbon round his neck because he is my birthday dog," said Kitty. So she tied a big red ribbon round the dog's neck and then took him out into the garden to play. Helen saw them and thought the little dog was a dear.

That afternoon many children came to the house next door, all dressed up for the party. Helen could hear them playing games in the big room at the back.

"I expect they will have tea in the dining-room at the front of the house," she thought to herself. "It will be laid there. Oh, I wonder if the curtains are drawn! If they aren't I could just peep in at the window and see that birthday cake!"

Helen slipped on her coat and ran down to see. No, the curtains were not drawn! What luck! The little girl tiptoed her way into the front garden next door and went up to the big window. She peeped in – and oh, what a lovely tea-table there was, just inside! You should have seen the cakes and buns, the biscuits and the jellies! And right in the very middle of the table was the birthday cake!

It was even lovelier than Helen had imagined. It was big, and was iced with pink and white sugar. On the top in the middle were five fairies, proper little dolls, not made of sugar, but dressed in silk, with silver wings. Each one carried a candle of a different colour!

Helen looked and looked – and then she saw something that made her open her eyes wide. The puppy had just run into the room. He stopped and smelled all the good things on the table. His brown nose twitched in excitement. What a lot of things to eat!

He jumped up on a chair and ate a plate of sandwiches – and then he saw that birthday cake. How he longed to lick it! Helen felt certain he was going to eat the cake, fairies and all, and she gave a scream. She rushed up the steps to the front door and hammered on it loudly. The children's mother opened it in surprise.

"Oh, please, Mrs White, your puppy is

just going to eat that lovely birthday
cake!" panted Helen. "I saw him through
the window!"

Mrs White rushed into the dining-room
and the puppy jumped off the table at

once. She looked at the birthday cake. One candle was broken – but the cake was all right! She saw the empty plate where the sandwiches had been and she smacked the puppy hard.

"Naughty little dog!" she said. "You must learn not to steal! You might have spoilt the party! I don't know what Kitty would have said if you had spoiled her cake. She would have cried her eyes out!"

She quickly put another candle in the place of the broken one, and before she went to the kitchen to make some more sandwiches she turned to speak to Helen. But the little girl had slipped out, rather frightened to find herself in the

big house, alone in a room with Mrs White.

"Dear me, bless the child, she's gone!" said Mrs White. "Funny little shy thing! Gillian! Gillian! Come here a minute, will you!"

Gillian came running in, her eyes bright with excitement. It was a lovely party. Her mother told her what had happened and how Helen had run off before she could be thanked.

"Shall we send her in a piece of the birthday cake, Gillian?" said Mrs White. "She always seems such a lonely little girl to me."

"Oh, Mummy, she must be a dear!" said Gillian. "Fancy coming in like that to save our birthday cake! Oh, Mummy, do let me go and bring her back to the party! We've always wanted to know her, she looks so sweet and kind, but she just looks away when we want to smile at her!"

"Very well," said Mrs White, smiling at her kindhearted little daughter. "Fetch her in – but she may not want to come,

Gillian, for I think her grandmother is very poor and I expect Helen has no party dress."

"Well, she can wear my old one, then!" said Gillian, dancing about in glee. "It will fit her nicely!"

Off she went to the little house next door and rang the bell. Helen opened the door, and stared in surprise at Gillian, all dressed up in silver and blue.

"Helen, thank you so much for saving our birthday cake!" cried Gillian. "Please, we want you to come to Kitty's birthday party, oh do, do, do! We've wanted to know you for a long time, but you wouldn't look at us!"

"Oh – I can't come," said Helen, blushing red. "I've no party dress."

"I've thought of that," said Gillian, taking hold of Helen's hand. "You can wear my old one, it's perfectly good except it's too small for me. Come on, I want you!"

"But-but-but," said Helen, simply longing to go, but feeling dreadfully shy.

"What are you saying so many buts

for?" cried her grandmother. "Go, child, go! It will do you good!"

So Helen went. Gillian gave her her old party dress of pink and it fitted Helen beautifully. Gillian found a pink ribbon which Helen tied in her hair, and then she slipped a pair of dancing shoes, which also belonged to Gillian, on her feet. Then she was ready. Down she went to the party, and soon everyone knew that she was the little girl who had saved the

birthday cake from being eaten.

What a fuss they made of her! It was such fun! They played games until tea-time and then they all went in to tea. The candles on the cake were alight and how lovely the five fairies looked, each holding one! Their silver wings glittered and their little faces shone in the candle-light. All the children cheered and Kitty went red with joy. It was the loveliest birthday cake she had ever had!

After tea there was the conjuror and he was very clever indeed. Then there was the bran-tub – and there was a present for Helen, though she hadn't expected one at all – and what do you think it was? Guess!

It was one of the fairies off the birthday cake! Helen couldn't believe her eyes. She looked at the beautiful little doll in delight – the nicest toy she had ever had!

"Oh thank you, Mrs White!" she said. "I do love it!"

"You deserve it!" said Mrs White, smiling. "Now, mind you come and play in the garden with Gillian, Mary and

Kitty whenever you can. They will love to have you, and you mustn't be lonely any more!"

So now Helen has three good friends and every day she plays in the garden next door. They have a lovely time, especially when Spot the dog joins them. Helen is very fond of him. "You see," she says, "if it hadn't been for Spot I'd never have known you all, would I?"

Clever Old
Shaggy

In the Long Field old Shaggy the cart-
horse lived by himself. He was a wise old
horse, and the farmer trusted him and
made a friend of him.

"You shall have a field to yourself," he
told Shaggy. "I won't put you in with
those skittish young horses, and the
three donkeys. They would only bother
you with their nonsense and their silly
ways."

Shaggy was glad not to be with the
others. The donkeys were stupid, and
the other horses were young and liked
chasing each other round and round the
field. Shaggy worked harder than any of
them, and he was tired at the end of the
day. He wanted to rest and be quiet.

But sometimes he would go to the

hedge and put his great brown head over to have a word with the others. His long tail would swish away the flies as he stood there.

The other horses and the donkeys were proud when Shaggy spoke to them. They thought he was very old and wise. They asked his opinion about all kinds of things.

"Do you think it is best to have a long tail like yours, or a docked tail, cut short and tied with a ribbon?" asked a vain young horse. "I should like mine docked. I saw a horse with a docked tail yesterday, tied up with a red ribbon. It looked so smart."

Shaggy made a loud, scornful hrrrumphing noise. "Don't you ever have your tail docked if you can help it! Have a bit of sense, Blossom! Think what you use your tail for!"

"Do I use it?" said Blossom, who was a very foolish young horse. "I just wave it to and fro, that's all."

"Well, just keep it still for a few minutes," said Shaggy. "Then you will know why you use it so much!"

So Blossom kept her tail quite still, and hundreds of flies ran joyfully over her back and tried to bite her. At once she swished her tail again.

"Oh, I know why I use my tail!" she cried. "It's to swish away the hundreds of flies that annoy me!"

Shaggy told the horses and donkeys

other things. He told them to stand with their backs to a storm of rain. He told them to shelter from the sun when it was too hot. He told them to bury their heads in the elderberry bushes when the flies were too bad, for insects did not like the strong elderberry smell.

"You are clever, Shaggy!" they all said. "We shall always come to you for advice. We do wish you lived in the same field as us – we would race you every night!"

Then Shaggy felt very glad that he did not live in the same field! He was always so tired at night after his long day in the fields, pulling the plough, or the hay-wagon, or the heavy farm carts. He went into the heaviest, muddiest fields, and

his shaggy ankles would be deep in the mud. Then he would have to strain and pull at the cart behind him, and get even deeper into the mud.

"Hey up, there, old Shaggy!" the farmer would say. "Hey up, there! Good old horse! You're worth any three of the others!"

Now one day there came to live at the cottages nearby four rough children from the town. They didn't know anything about the country. They didn't know enough even to shut gates after them when they went into the fields. They had come down for a holiday and they meant to enjoy it.

They threw stones at the ducks on the pond. They chased the hens that ran tamely about the lanes. They picked any fruit they could see, no matter who it belonged to. In fact they were a great nuisance, and the farmer frowned whenever he saw them.

Then the four children discovered that the donkeys and horses lived together in the nearby field. They swung on the gate and looked at them.

"Bet I could ride that pony!" said Tom, one of the big boys.

"Bet I could ride all the donkeys!" said Harriet. "I once rode one in a London park, and didn't I make it go when I whacked it with a stick!"

"Let's get sticks and catch a donkey or a horse each and ride them!" said Jack.

"Ooooh, let's!" said Rosie. So they all got big sticks from the hedge and then went into the field to catch a horse or a

donkey. All the animals were tame, and used to the farmer's children, so they let themselves be caught quite easily by the four town children.

But, oh dear, what a terrible time they had! They were made to canter round and round the field, and they had to gallop, too, when the children whacked them hard.

The horses and the donkeys panted and puffed. It was a hot evening, and all they wanted was to keep quiet and cool, somewhere away from the flies. But no, round and round the field they had to carry those four heavy children.

Shaggy watched them from the next field. He put his head over the hedge and saw all that was happening.

"Look at that great big horse!" said Tom. "I wish I could ride him! I bet I'd make him go! I'd whack him till he galloped at top speed!"

Shaggy heard what Tom said. He hrrumphed loudly and scornfully. What! Let a boy like that catch him and whack him? Not he!

All the horses and donkeys grumbled that night. They were sore from the whackings. They said they wouldn't let those children catch them another time.

"We'll run away each time they come near," said the donkeys, and the horses nodded, too.

But it wasn't so easy to run away from so many children, and soon the poor creatures were having to carry the four of them and their sticks once again. They saw Shaggy looking over the hedge, and they called to him. "What shall we do,

Shaggy? We are getting so tired!"

Now, the next night Shaggy jumped over the hedge and came into the field where the horses and donkeys lived. "You must all run away fast when those children come," he said. "But I will stay still. You can watch and see what I will do!"

"Here they come!" said the smallest donkey and ran to hide behind a tree. In came the children, leaving the gate open as usual. They ran to the horses, but in no time all the animals had scattered and were galloping away – all but old Shaggy.

He stood there, his head down, waiting. The children ran over to him. "Here's that big horse from the next field. Let's ride him! Two of us can get on his back together easily, he's so very big!"

"Hasn't he got shaggy ankles?" said Harriet. "I'll help you up, Tom. Now you, Rosie. Jack and I will have our turns next. Here are your sticks. Whack him hard."

Whack! The sticks made Shaggy jump.

Nobody had ever whipped him in his life and he didn't like it. He neighed angrily and started off towards the open gate. The children clung to him, Tom holding his mane and Rosie holding on to Tom.

He lumbered out of the gate. He lumbered down the lane. Tom and Rosie were delighted at their unexpected trip. Down the lane he went and round the corner.

Not far off was the farmer's duck-pond, with the ducks still swimming busily on it. Shaggy made his way towards it. *Whack!* Tom hit him hard with his stick again and made him jump. He ran a little faster. He ran faster still. He came right up to the duck-pond. And there Shaggy

stopped very suddenly indeed. He stopped
so unexpectedly that both Tom and Rosie
shot right over his head – and *splash*!
They flew into the duck-pond, scattering
the ducks in fright.

They shrieked and yelled as they tried to clamber out. They were so scared that they hardly knew what they were doing. The farmer's wife came out and saw them.

"So old Shaggy threw you in the pond, did he?" she said. "It'll do you a lot of good! No, it's no good asking me to dry and clean you. I've no use for badly behaved children like you! You go home to your aunt and let her scold you."

By this time old Shaggy was back at the field. He trotted in at the open gate and went to where Harriet and Jack were trying to corner one of the grey donkeys. He stood by patiently, his head drooping.

"Oh, here's the cart-horse back again, come to fetch us!" cried Jack in delight. "Come on, Harriet!"

And up on his back they got. *Whack*! What a big stick Jack had! Shaggy trotted heavily down the lane. He knew another place to put these two children. Not the pond this time! Oh, no! Somewhere else!

Shaggy knew a thick bed of nettles and blackberry bushes. The nettles stung sharply, and the blackberry sprays were set with curved prickles. Aha, Harriet and Jack, there is a treat in store for you!

Whack! Shaggy went a little faster, and Jack, delighted, whacked him again. Shaggy ran right into the thick nettles and brambles, for his thickly-haired legs felt no stings or thorns. He stopped very suddenly indeed. And over his head shot the two astonished children, straight into the nettles and brambles. How they howled and yelled!

"I'm stung! I'm stung!"

"The thorns are scratching me all over! Look at my dress. It's torn to bits. What will Auntie say?"

Shaggy didn't wait. He trotted back to his own field. He could hear the wailing voices of the children and then he heard the farmer's voice.

"Oho! So Shaggy tipped you in here, did he? You pair of ragamuffins, you deserve all you get. That'll teach you to tease my hens and stone my ducks. Be off with you!"

And then, up the lane, came four crying children. Tom and Rosie were muddy and wet through. Harriet and Jack were stung and scratched, and their clothes were torn. What would their aunt say?

All the horses and donkeys stood by the gate and watched them go by. Shaggy put his head over the hedge and watched, too.

"Nasty, unkind horse!" wept Harriet. "See what you've done to us! We'll never come near any of you again."

"Hrrrumph!" said all the horses. And the donkeys threw up their heads and laughed loudly.

"Hee-haw, hee-hee-haw, hee-hee-hee-haw!"

Shaggy was a clever old horse, wasn't he? He knew how to deal with naughty children all right!

The
Enchanted Book

This is an odd story. It is about John, a boy who lived in London fifty years ago. John is grown up now, of course, and he doesn't know if it was all a dream, or if it really happened. You must decide for yourself when you read the story.

John was eight years old. He was just an ordinary boy, going to school every day, working, playing, eating, and going to bed at night, just as you do.

He was naughty sometimes, just as you are. He was kind sometimes, just as you are. When he was naughty his mother and teachers scolded him. When he was kind they loved him. Sometimes they said: "You must be honest. You must be patient. You must be unselfish."

But they didn't tell him exactly *why*

he must. He thought about it a little, and then he said to himself, "I don't see that it matters very much if I tell a little lie now and again. No one will know. And if I buy sweets and eat them all myself, why shouldn't I? No one will know. And what does it really matter that I took Harry's rubber the other day and didn't give it back? He didn't know I took it. As long as nobody knows, I can't see that it matters."

And then one day something happened to him that showed him the real reason why all those things did matter.

At that time John was sort of half-and-half. That is, he sometimes told the truth, and he sometimes didn't. He was sometimes kind and sometimes unkind. He was sometimes quite honest, and sometimes not. A lot of children are like that. John could be very mean and spiteful and rough – but he could also be very generous and unselfish and gentle. He was just about half-and-half. Half good, and half bad.

Now one day, when he was still a half-

and-half, he went shopping by himself.
He went down an old, old street in
London, peering into shops that sold old,
old things. They were dusty, and they
looked sad and forgotten. There were
curious mirrors with dragons carved
round the frames. There were old china

ornaments – spotted dogs and funny cats, and some shepherdesses with sheep. There were old chairs, some of them so big that John half wondered if they had belonged to giant men.

He saw a dear little workbasket that had once belonged to an old lady many years ago. On the lid were two letters made of mother-of-pearl. They shone prettily. The letters were M.L. John stared at them, and a thought came into his head.

"M.L.," he said to himself. "Mother's name is Mary Lomond. What fun if I bought that basket for her birthday! I'll ask how much it is."

He went into the shop. The funniest old man came out of the dark part of the shop – rather like an old spider coming out of its web, John thought.

"How much is this basket, please?" asked John.

"Two pounds," said the old man.

John stood and thought. He had almost two pounds at home – but he had meant to buy himself a penknife with some of it. He badly wanted a penknife. All the boys in his class had a penknife except John. If he spent all his money on the basket, he wouldn't be able to have the penknife. So, after thinking for a while, John shook his head.

"I've only got about five shillings," he said. This wasn't true, but he didn't want to explain to the man that he almost had enough but wanted to spend some on himself. The old man nodded.

"Look around and see if there's anything else," he said. He hobbled off and left John in the untidy, musty, dusty old shop. The boy began to look round. He looked at a set of old games. He tried all the drawers in a funny old desk. He looked at some of the old books on a shelf.

And it was there he found what he always afterwards called the Enchanted Book. It was an enormous book, and the cover shone strangely, almost as if it were on fire. When he was looking at the cover the old shopman appeared again. "You'd better not look at that book," he said. "That's a dangerous book. It's got *you* in it."

John was startled. "What do you mean?" he said.

"It's a strange book," said the old man. "Anyone who looks well into it will see himself in the future. I wouldn't look, if I were you. You might not like what you see."

"Why not?" asked John, puzzled. "I'm going to be a doctor. I'd like to see what I look like as a grown-up doctor. I'm going to be a clever doctor. I'm not only going to make people well, I'm going to make a lot of money, too."

"I wouldn't look in that book if I were you," said the old man, and he tried to

take the book away. "Look here, my boy,
I'm old and I know a lot. You've got a
mouth that looks a bit hard to me. You've
a wrinkle over your eyes that tells me
you can be unkind. You've a look in your
eyes that tells me you don't always speak
the truth. Don't you look into that book.
You'll see something that will make you
afraid and unhappy."

177

Well, that made John feel he simply must see the pages of that book. He couldn't really believe that they would show him himself, but he felt that he must find out.

"I want to see," he said. "Please, do let me see. I won't damage the book in any way."

He looked up at the old man and smiled. Now John's smile was very nice. His eyes lit up, and creased at the corners, his mouth curved merrily, and his whole face changed. The old man looked at him closely.

"I believe you're half-and-half," he said. "If you are, this book will show you two stories with pictures – one story will begin at the beginning of the book. The other one you'll find by turning the book the other way and opening it at the end. If you're half-and-half – that is, half good and half bad – there's no harm in letting you see the book. All right. Have your own way. We'll open the book at this end first."

The old man opened the book and

178

John stared in great surprise – for there was a picture of himself, in jersey and short trousers, just as he was then.

"You," said the old man, and turned a page. "Here you are doing something you're ashamed of – ah, yes – cheating at sums. Dear, dear, what a pity! And here you are boasting about something you hadn't really done. And look – what's this picture? You're bigger here – about two years older, I should think. You are telling an untruth without even going red! You're winning a prize, but only because you told that untruth."

"I don't like this book," said John, and he tried to close it. The old man stopped him.

"No. Once you've opened it, you've got to go on. Look at this picture – you're quite big here. You're being unkind to a smaller boy – but there's no one to see, so you don't mind. Nasty little bully! And oh, look here – who's this? Your mother?"

"Yes," said John. "Why is she crying in the picture?"

"Because she's so disappointed in you," said the old man. "Look, it's her birthday – she's got a birthday card in her hand. She wanted you to spend her birthday with her, and you had promised to but at the last moment somebody asked you to go to a picnic and you went there instead. You didn't really mind if your mother was sad or not. She's thinking about you – feeling disappointed that you are growing up into a selfish, boastful, unkind youth."

"I don't like that picture," said John, in a trembling voice. "Turn the page, quick."

The page turned. "Why, here you're grown up!" said the old man. "Fine-looking fellow, too. You're studying to be

a doctor. You said you meant to be one, didn't you? Well, you are going to be. This man here in this picture with you is saying that to be a doctor is a wonderful thing – you can bring healing and happiness to people who need it. But you are laughing and saying: 'That's all very well, I'll do that all right – but I'll be a rich man, too. I'll make people pay all I can.'"

John said nothing. He didn't like himself at all in the pictures. The old man turned to him. "You mustn't be surprised at what you see," he said gravely. "After all, you tell stories now – you are sometimes hard and unkind –

you are not always honest and I can see you are often selfish. Well, those things grow, my boy, they grow – and this is what they grow into!"

The pages turned again. John saw himself getting older and older. He saw himself getting rich. He saw himself with a pretty wife – with happy children. He saw himself getting older still, and his face was not pleasant. It was hard and selfish.

He saw himself being pleasant to rich people, and rough with poor ones. He

saw himself cheating when he could do it without being found out. He saw himself being bad-tempered at home, and unkind to the children. And then, alas, came some dreadful pictures, when he had been found out in some wrong-doing, and had lost all his money! His children left home when they were old enough, because they hated him; and his pretty wife grew ugly and bad-tempered because she was lonely and unhappy.

"I hate this book!" cried John. The pictures had come to an end. The old man turned the book round the other way and opened the pages from the end instead of the beginning.

"Wait," he said. "I told you you were a half-and-half, didn't I? We'll see what the other half of you might lead to."

And there, page by page, was the story of what would be John's life if the good half of him grew, instead of the bad.

You should have seen those pictures! He won prizes, not by cheating, but by hard work. He gained friends, not by boasting, but by kindness. His mother smiled out from the story, happy in an unselfish and loving son. There he was, studying to be a doctor, but this time not boasting that he meant to be rich. This time he was saying something else. "The world is divided into two kinds of people – the ones who help and the ones who have to be helped. I'm going to be one who helps. I don't care if I make money or not – but I do care if I make happiness."

And there was his wife again – and his happy children. But this time they loved him, gave him a great welcome whenever he came home. They hadn't so much money – but how proud they were of John. How the sick people loved him, and how happy he was. His face was not so hard as in the other pictures. It was kind and happy. It was the face of a great and a good man.

"Well, there you are," said the old man, shutting the book up softly. "You're a half-and-half, as I said. Let the bad half of you grow, and it will grow into a bad man. Let the good half grow, and you'll

get plenty of happiness and give it to others as well. Ah, my boy, there's a reason for not telling fibs, for not being dishonest, for not being unkind, for not cheating, for not being mean. We've all got the choice when we're small of letting one half of ourselves grow, or the other half. Nobody else but ourselves can choose."

"Yes," said John, in a small voice.

"You may think to yourself, 'Nobody knows I'm telling a fib,'" said the old man. "But *you* know it. That's what matters. It makes the wrong half grow, you see. Well, my boy, you'd better get back home now. And never mind about that workbasket. I can easily sell it to someone else if you haven't enough money."

"I have enough money," said John. "At least, I shall have tomorrow, when Father gives me my Saturday money. That was really a fib I told. I wanted a penknife, you see. But now I am going to spend the whole of my money on that basket for my mother's birthday."

"Take it with you now," said the old man, "and you can bring me the money tomorrow."

"Will you trust me, then?" asked John. "I told you a fib just now, you know."

"I'll trust you," said the old man. "Go along, little half-and-half. Here's the basket."

John went, full of wonder and very puzzled. A good many things were suddenly very clear to him. He saw now why it mattered so much whether he chose to do wrong things or right things. He had to make himself, good or bad.

The man he was going to be would be exactly as he made him. It was the little things, the right and wrong things he did, that were going to lead to all sorts of big things.

That isn't quite the end of John's story. He's a great doctor now, the kindest and most honest man you could meet. He says that the strange Enchanted Book told him things every child ought to know.

"Most children are half-and-half," he says. Well – I expect you are, too, aren't you? Choose the right half, whatever you do, and let it grow. I can't show you the Enchanted Book, because I don't know where it is now, but if ever I find it, we'll look at it together. I wonder what it will show us!